AUSSIE BIG ACHIEVERS

STEVE IRWIN

written by RICHARD SIMPKIN

illustrated by DEBRA O'HALLORAN

Other AUSSIE BIG ACHIEVERS books
CATHY FREEMAN
ASH BARTY
SHANE WARNE

We acknowledge the Traditional Owners of the land on which we publish books, the Quandamooka people and pay our respects to Elders past, present and emerging.

Disclaimer

The information in this book is true and complete to the best of our knowledge.

All recommendations are made without any guarantee on the part of the author, illustrator and publisher, who also disclaim any liability incurred in connections with the use of this data or specific details.

This publication has not been prepared, approved or licensed by the individual that it has been written about. It also hasn't been approved or licensed by the individual's management. This is not an official publication.

Published by:
Boolarong Press,
38/1631 Wynnum Road
Tingalpa Qld 4173
Australia.
www.boolarongpress.com.au

First published 2021

A catalogue record for this book is available from the National Library of Australia

ISBN: 9781922643162 (Paperback)

Printed and bound by Watson Ferguson & Company, Tingalpa, Australia

DEDICATION

This book is dedicated to You,
because You can achieve any dream You have!

Steve Irwin was born in Victoria on the 22 February 1962, which was also his mum's birthday!

When Steve was eight his family moved to Queensland and his mum and dad opened the Beerwah Reptile Park.

Steve grew up surrounded by animals; his mum looked after orphaned and injured animals. His dad was a wildlife expert. Steve loved all kinds of animals, but his favourites were reptiles.

It wasn't unusual for the family home to have kangaroos, koalas, birds and even snakes, all living together in their house.

Can you imagine how much fun that would have been for Steve?

When Steve was just nine, he started helping his dad catch crocodiles to relocate them.

Steve's dad taught him that you could relocate crocodiles in a safe way so that no one would get hurt, including the crocodiles.

Steve loved helping his mum and dad everyday at their wildlife park where he would feed and look after the animals. As he was always around animals, he not only loved them, but he was continuously learning about them. Steve was also learning about the environment and how it was not only important to the animals; it was equally important to us all.

Steve loved animals so much that he used to get his mum to stop the car on the way to school if he saw any animals that needed rescuing.

After Steve had finished school, he continued to work at his family's reptile park.

He also spent time catching crocodiles in remote Queensland and would move them to a safer location. Steve used to take his video camera with him to film his adventures with the "crocs" and dreamed of one day showing everyone how amazing "crocs" are. Steve loved to tell people that "Crocs Rule".

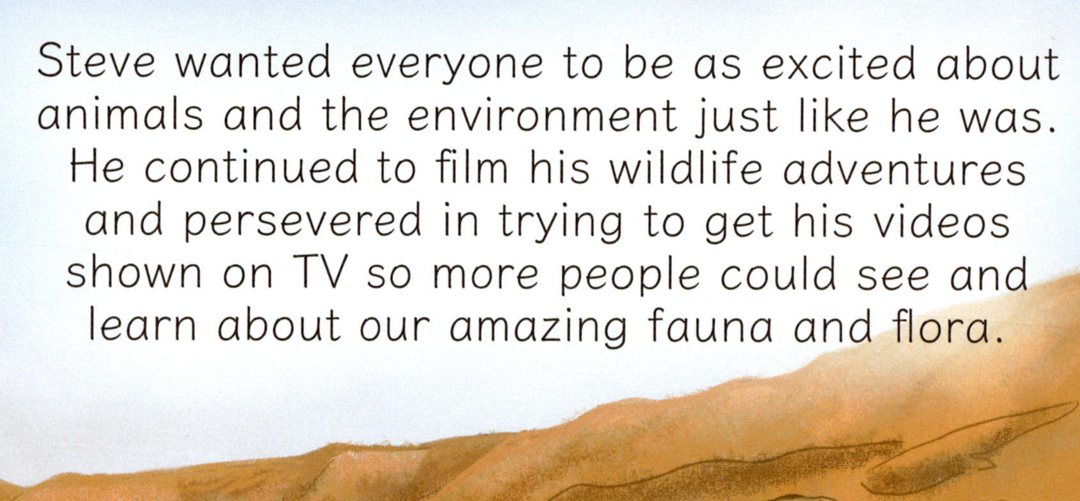

Steve wanted everyone to be as excited about animals and the environment just like he was. He continued to film his wildlife adventures and persevered in trying to get his videos shown on TV so more people could see and learn about our amazing fauna and flora.

CRIKEY!

In 1996, one of Steve's dreams came true, his TV show called "The Crocodile Hunter" was shown in Australia and the following year it was shown in North America and the United Kingdom. The Crocodile Hunter was so popular that over 500 million people watched it in over 130 countries. "CRIKEY" that's a lot of people!

As Steve was so enthusiastic about the wildlife and the environment, millions of kids that watched his TV show all wanted to be just like Steve — a wildlife warrior.

In 1998, Steve changed the name of the reptile park to Australia Zoo. He continued to film his TV show and even appeared in Hollywood movies. Steve was able to buy lots of land in Australia and other parts of the world so that he could protect the animals that lived on the land. He also protected the land for future generations.

Australia Zoo is still very popular and people from Australia and around the world visit the zoo, which is managed by Steve's wife Terri and his two children, Bindi and Robert. Steve taught his children to treat every living being with kindness.

Steve's love and respect for wildlife, the environment and global conservation is something that we should all strive for and if we do, we can all become "Wildlife Warriors" just like Steve.

FUN QUESTIONS

[1] What member of Steve's family does he share his birthday with?

[2] What animals did Steve have in his house when he was growing up?

[3] How old was Steve when he started helping his dad catch crocodiles?

[4] What did Steve love to tell people about crocs?

[5] What was the name of Steve's TV show called?

[6] What is the name of Steve's zoo?

[7] What did Steve's two children learn from their dad?

[8] Steve was also known as a Wildlife… ?

[9] In your opinion what can you do to become a Wildlife Warrior?

ABOUT THE AUTHOR

Richard Simpkin was born in Sydney, Australia in 1973 and has worked as a photographer in Australia, England and the US for 25 years.

He is a best-selling author of five books, two of which are about Australian legends who he met, photographed and interviewed.

In 2014 Richard also founded World Letter Writing Day and has inspired children and adults all around the world to take a break from social media and write handwritten letters.

Richard has also conducted many workshops at schools in Australia. The students often ask him about many of the Australian legends that he has met over the years. This has inspired Richard to create these fun yet educational books about iconic Australians who we should all know about.

Other books by author

Australian Legends, 2005
Richard and Famous, 2007
100 Australian Legends, 2014
Michael in Pictures, 2015
Richard Simpkin Celebrity Quotes, 2016
Cathy Freeman — Aussie Big Achievers, 2021
Ash Barty — Aussie Big Achievers, 2021
Shane Warne — Aussie Big Achievers, 2022

OTHER AUSSIE BIG ACHIEVERS BOOKS

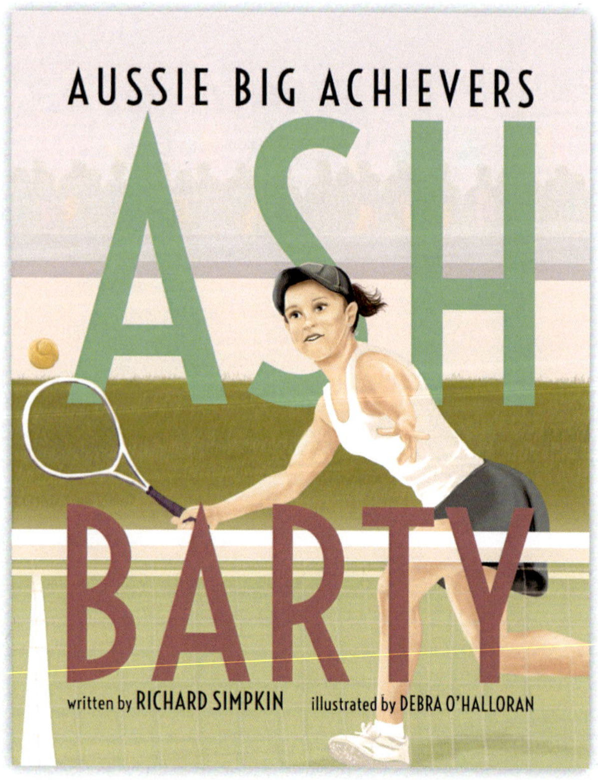

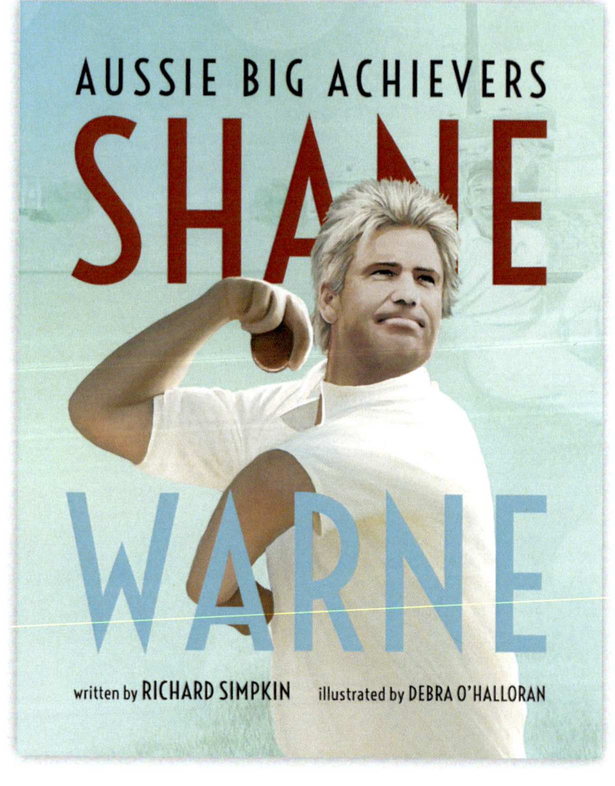